A CRAZY KIND OF URGENCY

A Crazy Kind Of Urgency

Copyright 2021 by Kimberly Westrope

This is a work of fiction created by the
author and belonging solely to the author.
ISBN 978-1-7324598-1-6
Pub. Date December 2021

daisy fields press

Cover design and photo: Kimberly Westrope
Author photo: Tessa Thewes Photography

Thank you to my editor, Carolee Moore, for being my first reader, critic, encourager, sister, and friend.
Thank you to all my readers, past, present, and future. I hope my words touch your hearts.
Thank you, Heavenly Father, for giving me the ability to put my thoughts onto paper, and for fulfilling my dreams of doing so. All glory to You.

Dedicated to J.N.
the one who mattered most

Other Books by Kimberly Westrope

<u>Love On the Mountaintop inspirational series:</u>

Brother's Keeper (book #1)

<u>Historical Romance</u>

The Earl's Masquerade

<u>Poetry Collections</u>

Dancing On Borders
The Prints of All My Days
White Flag In the Wind

A
CRAZY KIND
OF URGENCY

Kimberly Westrope

daisy fields press

Temecula, CA

Table of Contents

AWAITING YOUR ARRIVAL

Many modes of
transportation,
travelers seeking
destination,
wanderers on epic quests
searching for their grail.

The bench beneath me is
permanent,
moored as it is,
encased in cement.
I wonder if you'll even
notice me in your rush
to be somewhere.

I'm the one with the red
bandana
and a copy of Keats in my
hand;
The one with hopeful eyes
surreptitiously scanning
the crowd.

If you take a moment to pause,
in the causeway,
glancing around,
wondering if you've forgotten
something
or why you are even here,

If your eyes find
their way to mine,
and there is a sudden
stop in time,
a smile will tell me
you've come
to find me here,
awaiting your arrival.

CRUSH(ED)

Crush

···beneath the gaze of the
beloved,
my breathe leaves me.
Gasping,
I struggle to move,
finding my feet firmly
fettered.
Eyes press into me,
searching the depths of me;
I tremble beneath the weight
of their stare.

···because no words come
forth
from my paralyzed
vocal cords,
nor does a sound from the
beloved come.

My thoughts run rampant,
none of them slowing,
nor gathering
together to form sentences.
My ears suffer the loss in the
deafening silence.
···before the lips can
form words,
because the smile is
welcoming,
beckoning, in a language
I think I know,
but don't quite understand,
I wait for clarity to come
somewhere
in the translation.

···behind the wall of doubt,
despairing;
neither of us knows how to
climb so high,
fearing that time's end is
running nigh.

I ache, I pine, I perish
for the one
who has secretly, silently
become my···

Crush.

HE AND SHE

He appears quite suddenly;
She is unprepared.
He steps from shadows into
sunlight;
She melts in the heat.
He speaks in words
she can't understand;
She stands, speechless,
before him.
His voice drips, honey-like,
into her ears;
She tastes every syllable.
His eyes are azure skies
enveloping her;
She walks on clouds.
His gaze holds her
from across the room;
She feels the flutter of
eyelashes.
He stirs things deep inside
her;
She longs to set them free.

He is everything her heart
has hoped for;
She trembles with the
longing.
His touch is a soft flame;
She is ignited from the inside.
He is unaware of the scar
 he leaves;
She will never be the same.

FULL MOON

You crept into my universe.
The night sky held you,
hovering in my atmosphere,
ever near, every part,
never far from me.

Your satin surface
reached for me,
and held me in your
tender touch.
It was too much for me;
I couldn't find my footing.

Your radiance enraptured me,
in captive awe.
I gathered you near and
tried to hold on.
Alas, you slipped away
with the dawn.

Sometimes I still see you
there,
far away and out of reach,
held in a dream or a memory,
frozen in time for
safekeeping.

A yearning, a dream,
or a distant memory,
you were real to me
when I held you,
burning, in my hands and
in my heart;
The embers are still
alive in your eyes.

DARK EYES AND CARELESS HAIR

You find me in the shadows.
With your dark eyes and
careless hair,
you seek me out,
and pull me in.
You must carry
some kind of magnet
that draws me ever near.

I have no power of resistance,
no desire to disengage.
You hold me
in the palm of your hand,
the lightest touch, and yet,
I feel myself bending
to your will.

Take me as I am for what
I am is yours.
I've waited a lifetime for
this.

Entangled, bewitched,
and smitten besides,
I couldn't stop this if I tried.

I am undone, falling, falling.
The closer I get,
the further I fall,
So catch me if you can.
I crumble as I tumble
into your paradise
of careless hair and those
dark, dark eyes.

I LOVED YOU ONCE

Somewhere in town
I may have seen you,
sunlight whispering
upon your skin;
Glimpses of you,
hastily caught,
catching me of guard,
quickening my breath.

I may have tried to call
out to you,
hoping you would hear
my heart;
Maybe I stood,
paralyzed by your smile
and the uncertainty it
brought.

I am certain you stealthily
snuck into my dreams,
and most of my thoughts,
day and night.

I found no way to rid myself
of you, and yet no way to
make you mine.

Perhaps I'll hold you here
still,
as my words find their way to
these writings, wary and
weary
of wondering what is true,
and what needs to be left
behind.

I can say for sure I
loved you once,
however brief it may have
been,
that day I saw you on the
street,
and left my heart there
at your feet.

I MEANT TO SAY

Weak−kneed, I stumble
at the sight of you,
two left feet suddenly mired.
Myriad emotions
move through me,
scattering, wild as dreams,
unfettered, unfounded,
unsounded, unsaid.

I fumble for words
that tumble from my tongue,
landing in a heap,
there at my feet,
hitting hard
on the cracked cement.
Down through the cracks,
into the abyss, they fall
forever into darkness
and are gone.
I'll never retrieve them now.

No one will ever know
what they were meant to say.

Wordlessly, I turn away,
wondering why I even try.
Why does it have to be
so hard to be heard?
Why is silence never enough?

There has to be
 a common ground
where we can find ourselves
and let it be, let us just be
whatever we are meant to be.
Do me a favor, please?
If you find it, this place,
meet me there someday.

MEMORY

It flickers violently in
the recess of my mind,
silently taking me to another
place in time;
A moving picture show of
blurred images,
a black and white likeness
of what used to be.

The tender smile that
once caressed
is lost behind the
smoke and mirrors;
A sleight of hand,
a slight farewell···
I'd like to hold you,
but I've forgotten how,

and everything I thought I
knew,
all that I could understand,
lost comprehension

when you spoke
the words of a guilty man.

In the chilly air surrounding
me,
I search for the source
of warmth.
The embers, once kindled
in my soul,
scatter and fall into
the memory of you.

IN THE MIDST

I still remember your touch,
Your voice, your laughter;
It's all tucked away here
in the hollows of my heart.

A bit of you, a bit of me,
locked away in memories;
If ever you think of those
days,
I hope you know I loved you.

There is, even still,
a small spark,
a glowing ember that
ever lingers,

longingly, lovingly,
In the midst of
all these memories;

A candle kept on the
windowsill,
a hearth fire that
smolders still,
a warm heart
waiting to be held,
a blanket of love covers you.

THE BURDEN OF TIMID LOVE

You turned blind eye
and mute lips
away from me;
No words would be offered
to me on this day,
But as you turn away,
I see···what?
A lingering longing, desire,
hope that I might
today possess a new bravery
with which to reach out to
you,
to steady you in your
fumbling
and mumbling efforts at
intercourse?
I cannot,
for I am just as clumsy
and awkward
at such things.

Though my heart longs for it,
and my voice silently
cries out,
I find myself unable to move,
unable to rise and meet this
call to action.
My feet remain harbored
in the mire
that quickly and quietly
holds me captive;
A field of quicksand
between us,
a vacant bridge I cannot
cross.
What bravery I may have
fleetingly possessed
has faltered and vanished
amidst mixed signals and
mixed emotions throughout
years of such encounters.

So many wasted minutes,
hours, days;

years of frustration and
guilt.
Why can't I be the strong one
and see this through to
fruition?
What will be will be, it is
said,
but without forward motion,
life and love both grow
stagnant,
even toxic.
What miracle elixir
is there, then, for us?
I am at a loss to know.
I search your eyes again
for a signal,
some sure sign
to continue on this path.
I have so much
I want to give you,
if you'd only let it be.
This love is a burden I bear.

YOU DON'T SAY

You don't say the words
I long to hear,
you never speak my name.
Sometimes you don't even
utter hello
when I pass you in the café.

What once was new
and full of hope
is lost in this
symphony of silence
that echoes through the
chasm
stretched between us.

I can't build a bridge
on my own,
my words are too faulty a
foundation,
and I don't trust my voice
in its trembling.

If you find you can't help me,
I understand; It's a big task,
and
we're each made differently
(Though I suspect we're more
alike than not).

If you don't mind, though, I
think
I'll keep you as my muse,
for neither you nor I
can control
where the heart wanders.

I will hold on to fond
memories
full of smiles and blue eyes,
and sighs,
dreaming of all the words
that yet remain unspoken.

THE UNIVERSE RECLINING IN YOUR HAIR

The universe reclining
in your hair,
Dark as midnight, soft as air,
draws me ever closer still
to the magic I find hidden
there.

The twilight of heaven
in your eyes,
diamonds in a darkened sky,
glistening, glowing, drowning
pools of pleasure and delight.

The taste of love in your
smile,
as guileless as a child;
I knew it was meant for me,
and it held me there for a
while.

Never my lover,
forever my love,
I've held you here in my trove
of valuable and
delightful things,
quiet and precious as a dove.

I fall back into my memories,
every February the
thirteenth.
Recalling a touch, a smile, a
summer night…
I find you in all of these.

I seek, I find you,
I keep you there,
with all my treasures,
beautiful and rare,
to take out and hold
and remember…
the universe reclining
in your hair.

BENEATH THE HANDS OF THE MINSTREL

Soft sounds swayed
in melodious waves
across the moonlit mountain.
Stars shining brightly
lit up the skies,
hovering above the lovely
tune.

Standing silhouette on the
stage,
the music he played
filled a space in me
with humility, and hope.
I was honored to be placed
within his presence,
within those indulgent
notes and tones.

So close to me,
he was yet miles away
till his eyes found mine

in the crowd
and offered a sweet caress,
a slight nod, a smile,
though no words were
forthcoming.

As I watched and listened,
I held him in my heart,
Though my hands
could never reach him,
could never draw him
close enough.
Still, I swooned
under the hypnotic hands
of the minstrel;

Hands that coaxed such sweet
chords from the instrument
he held, hands that
mesmerized me,
blinded me with their beauty,
touched me deeply,
even without so much
as a fingertip's touch.

Every night I appeared,
and I watched him there,
drawn like a moth to a flame,
always keeping safe enough
distance,
hoping I wouldn't get burned,
but his ember eyes
always found me
as closer and closer,
he called to me
in hushed tones and
whispered words.
Finally, I found my way to
him,
succumbing in awe and
wonder.

Words were rushed,
faces flushed,
in heady conversation,
my giddy heart beside itself
in ebullient exhilaration.
I fell into forever dreams and
rested for a while

in the peace—embedded
mountain pines,
the heavy—leaden winter
skies,
rain—drenched days
and blazing nights,
blanketed with snow,
comforted and warm,
contented and calm
beneath the hands of the
minstrel.

THE WEIGHT OF A WHISPER

It's there,
in the depth of your stare,
in the unfettered readiness
of your smile,
in the silken touch that
shocks
and weakens me.
I feel it pulse
in the air around me.
Even without the words,
I know it is there,
trying to be heard
through the clamor,
longing for one to listen.
If you could let it go···
If I could find a way
to reach out,
meeting in the middle,
we would know
the weight of it.
It's the weight of a whisper
that yearns to be heard,

pressing into the fabric
of the earth,
waiting to be woven
into something
greater than each of us
standing alone,
raving to be claimed, reborn,
and held wholly formed···
a whisper into words.

YOU ARE THE MOUNTAIN
(I CAN'T CLIMB)

I see the skies in your eyes,
calling me to a higher place.
I feel the warmth
of a thousand suns
when that smile lights your
face.
The wind, it whispers and
echoes in my ear.
This is the music I hear
when you are near.
The ember flares,
and flames ignite
whenever you stand so close,
scorching my skin,
burning within,
consuming me in the smoke.

I clutch, I claw,
I scream, I crawl,
clinging to all that
 I thought I saw.

A bit of your heart,
a bit of hope
carried me up the mountain,
a beautiful sight.
In bright starlight,
I came to drink from the
fountain,
the water that cools,
the smile that soothes,
the aching finally abating.
I reached the crest,
a personal best,
but I find I'm not up to
the taking.
Too weak to move,
mired in the mud,
I would reach for you now
if I could.

A PART OF YOU

It's here in my heart,
hidden and hardened
like a calcium deposit
or a piece of petrified wood.

Sometimes it feels like a
hole,
a space that needs filling.
Sometimes it's like a
millstone
around my neck.

It's something I can't get rid
of,
no matter how I try.
I feel it there always,
a memento I can't throw away.

I tried to leave it behind,
keep what's passed in the
past,

memories locked up tight
in a box at the back
of my bureau.

The closest I came was
refusing to speak your name
and putting all the words
I had for you on paper.

I locked it all away
for another day, another
time and place, when
I might see you face to face

and give it back.
It's a small part of you
that you forgot to take when
you turned and walked away.

27 SECONDS

A lot can happen in 27
seconds.

A slow tear starts
in the corner of my heart,
wordlessly ripping me apart.
a life wholly changed,
memories rearranged,
leaving me a little deranged.
I fall away frowning,
feeling as if I'm drowning,
a new life now crowning –
Me without you, evermore.
All about you that I once
adored
takes 27 seconds to walk out
the door.

TENNIS BRACELET

I found a tennis bracelet
on the front seat of your car.
When I asked who
it belonged to,
you said it was for me.

I knew it couldn't be true.
You know a tennis bracelet's
not my style,
but you smiled and kissed me
and clasped it on my wrist.

It felt like a shackle
you placed there
to buy my silence and
quell my questions.
You acted like everything
was fine
while my world fell apart.

THREE TIMES
Ace Hotel –
You were there.
I saw you.

ACE HOTEL (6/29/19)

That beautiful old hotel
on Broadway in L.A.;
So many memories
held within its hallowed
halls,
patterned paper,
paper thin walls.

The music, the laughter,
the noise from the bar,
the boys in the band
rehearsing next door,
all sound so pure.

I remember fondly
that night that was filled
with an anticipating air;
The bursting rhythm,
the soulful songs,
singing along.
Passion and plundering,
wondering, wishing,

ever hopeful
that time would stand still
just for a moment.

I remember you fondly,
I remember you well;
A night worth remembering,
and the man left standing
at the Ace Hotel

BLAKE FALLS

Birthday cake and candles,
and a Penny to celebrate.
Like a sickness, it descends,
suddenly and without shame.
Happily, he reached for it,
taking the short way 'round,
taking the pain,
taking the rain,
taking the right way now.

A dozen red roses lie waiting
for the one whole stole
his heart.
"It was meant to be this way,"
he said. "My heart is whole
and full, though my body
trembles like a phantom."
The wait is over now,
the weight's been lifted.
No longer alone, together,
no longer two, but one.

24 SEVEN

I wait...
For that one small moment
when you look my way.
A brightness warms your eyes,
and your smile is just for me.
It's a small thing,
but it fills me, and I am
no longer empty.

BURNING DOWN THE HOUSE

First the smolder,
then the catch,
the scorch and blaze,
a bloom of fire: orange,
and the flickering blue heat
that draws me in.

HALLOWED HALLS

I walk the halls where your
footfalls
once followed me.
I visit vacant corridors
and wonder where you've gone.
A darkness descends
in the corners
of my hollowed heart.
Echoes of yesterday resonate
within its walls,
whispering your name
and daring me to call out;
I try, but there is no reply,
no sign of life.

BLACK–HAIRED BOYS AND
THOSE WHO MADE ME SMILE

I fell in love with
a black–haired boy
when I was seventeen.
His Irish eyes smiled on me,
green as any fertile field
along the western coast of
Ireland.

He had the gift of blarney,
as well, inherited
from his father's fathers,
and all the charm
that could do such harm
should it ever be left
unfettered.

So I gave him my heart;
Not what he wanted, but
he held it for a while,
nonetheless.

The parting sorrow
was mine only –
he never cared enough
to mind the loss.

Black–haired boy, the second,
was one more trusted and
true.
Even when I gave him
nothing to hold on to,
he held fast anyway,
grasping with a feather's
touch.
Gasping, I fell into his
Aquarian eyes,
and floated away,
unable to breathe,
to speak, or even to move;
Afraid of the strength
of such a love.

Clowns and poets,
friends and foes –
young love held captive

in my closet,
tied up tightly with a neat
bow,
and a gag thrust in its mouth.
I'll hear no words from you
tonight –
no promises never to be
fulfilled,
no unclaimed emotions
being stirred uselessly.

I'll never speak the
words that hang
heavy on my tongue,
for what's done is done,
and will be no more,
except in solemn
remembrance
and in these paltry poems
that hold all I longed to say···
and more.

You were loved,
of that I am sure

each and every one,
a young girl's dream.
You are remembered,
mostly fondly,
For making me laugh
so hard I cried,
for making me cry
so hard I thought
I would never smile again.
I smile now most of the time.
My memories of you
are mainly good ones.
I hope that you
can say the same.

EVELYN'S LOVE   6/5/19
(for Evelyn, whose young
husband of just three months
was killed by a drunk driver)

I reach for you in the half—
dawn,
knowing you're not there.
My heart still hurts
anew each morn,
finding you gone.
I mourn again with fresh
tears.

My fingers
linger on your pillow,
now ever cold to my touch.
It hurts too much
to raise my head,
to raise myself
to face the days without you.

Gone too soon, I hardly had
time to know you,
to love you as I longed to.
No future for us now;
My future, alone, looms,
a vast emptiness
you once filled.

Find me here, love,
and fill me once again.
I need to feel your presence
to feel whole again, to keep
moving forward,
one sad, slow step at a time,
till I greet you again
in eternity.

THE EYES HAVE SPOKEN

The eyes have always
had much to say
when words on the tongue
lay unspoken;
Eyes that held in their
deep see depths
oceans of longing and
hopes never met.
Brown eyes, too, in their
chocolatey hues,
Melted me with a fire
from within.

The Irish eyes shone
emerald green,
all the while weaving
webs of deceit.
The black—eyed boy
with raven hair
Spoke mostly truth
and brought great joy.
Grey eyes grew cloudy,

causing confusion.
I never knew what they
were trying to say.

Some spoke lies,
and some spoke love,
Close by my side or
distanced afar,
windows wide open or
broken in pain,
Some were so closed
I could never get in.
Where words could not
or would not come,
the eyes have always spoken.

FEBRUARY

February dawns again,
drowning me in memories,
plying me with possibilities
of what might have been.
The month of love loves me
not,
for every thirteenth day
uncovers another
long—lost memory
of a love I never outgrew.
Nor could I grow toward you,
my arms stretched
like a flower
trying to reach the sun⋯
an impossibility.
The words wouldn't come,
though they sat
like lead on my tongue.
I could not form them into
any kind of gift to give you.
Your presence, never
wavering,

patiently waiting,
was more a gift to me
than you know.
Longing, lingering like
melted chocolate in your
eyes,
seared me with its intensity.
I never knew a love like that
could be kindled just for me.
I was too afraid of the fire
to draw close to the ember.

This February,
while lovers and others
are pledging fidelity,
I will remain loyal to a love
 mired in memories.

MOVING FORWARD

Hands hang useless at my
sides,
feet bound in debris,
pushing, pulling
through the mire,
no progress can be made,
only aching muscles
and an aching heart remain.

I can't reach you
where you are,
though I've tried
everything I know.
The lifeline offered
has been denied;
You carry the noose
around your neck,
waiting for the fall.

I reach to the sky for the
dove of peace,
hoping you'll hear its cry,

hunting for a harbor,
a place to land,
a safe place to sleep at night.

I labor on, with my heart
in my hand,
a billion broken pieces,
hoping to build the bridge
that mends
and binds us across the
chasm.

ABOUT THE AUTHOR

Kimberly Westrope grew up in Phoenix, AZ and has been writing poetry since elementary school. She lives in Southern California where she likes to spend her time reading, writing, crafting, and hanging out with her grandkids.

Kimberly has also published two romance novels, *Brother's Keeper* and *The Earl's Masquerade*. This is her third published book of poetry. Her other poetry collections are *Dancing On Borders*, *The Prints Of All My Days*, and *White Flag In the Wind*.

Before you go...

If you enjoyed this book, please leave a brief review on Amazon and/or Goodreads.
Amazon link:
https://www.amazon.com/s?k=kimberly+westrope&ref=nb_sb_noss

I would very much appreciate it. Thank you in advance.
I would also love to hear from you.
You can contact me at
kimberly.westrope@gmail.com

https://www.facebook.com/kimberly.westrope.5

http://kimberlywestropeauthor.wordpress.com/